My Dad Is A Superhero

Lily Lexington

IMPROVIGY PTY LTD
• SYDNEY, AUSTRALIA •

My Dad is a Superhero.

Sometimes when I don't want to go to bed, he flies me into my room! I soar through the air and land on my bed!

What fun we have together.

My Dad has x-ray vision.

When we play hide and seek, he always knows where I am hiding, even under the bed or in the closet!

My Dad always sees me no matter how quiet I am.

My Dad can hold his breath longer than anyone else. When we go to the swimming pool, he swims under water and throws me up into the air. Sometimes I can't find him because he can stay under for so long.

If there was a person stuck at the bottom of the swimming pool, my Dad could swim down and save them, with only one breath.

My Dad has super strength. When we go to the zoo, and it is hard for me to walk, my Dad can carry me on his shoulders as long as I need him to.

While I am up there I can see everything at the zoo. One time, I was as tall as the giraffe! Another time, a bird landed on my head.

My Dad is faster than a speeding bullet. One time when I fell off of my bike, my Dad ran to help me before I could even cry. He picked me up and put me back on my bike.

I kept trying, and before I knew it I was riding! My Dad had to use his super speed to keep up with me.

My Dad has sonic hearing. When I told my toys that I was not going to clean them up, my Dad heard me and made me clean them up anyway.

It was not very much fun cleaning up the mess that I had made, but after my dad heard me with his sonic hearing, he helped me and it was fun talking to him.

My Dad can read minds. One time when my Dad had to work late, he called me during dinner. When he asked me if I had eaten my vegetables and I did not answer he said, "I know that you have not eaten them!"

I gobbled them up and he said, "Now they are gone!"

It was so much fun.

My Dad can fly. The time that I talked to my dad on the phone, he told me he was in China. I asked him when he was coming home, and he told me he was flying home the next day. He was home when I got back from school.

I knew that he was fast but that was amazing.

My Dad can predict the future. When we were at my baseball game, and it was my turn to bat, my Dad told me that he knew I would get a big hit. I went up to bat and...

HOMERUN!

My Dad knew what was going to happen!

My Dad has elasticity. That means that he can stretch out as far as he needs to.

One time my sister wanted him to come into her room. But my Dad was playing with me. So I hung on to his arm and my sister did too.

No matter how hard we pulled, he just kept stretching!

My Dad can be invisible. One time I forgot to do my homework. When I went to school I told my teacher that the dog ate it.

My Dad was not there, but I heard him telling me to tell my teacher the truth. So I did.

Sometimes I wish that he did not have this power.

My Dad never gets hurt. When my Dad had to get surgery, he came home and played with me the next day.

There were stitches in his tummy, but they didn't hurt. Not even when I sat on his lap.

My Dad does not sleep, even after I go to bed, my Dad stays up and watches TV.

He does this so that he can protect our house. It is hard for him to stay up all of the time, so once in a while he takes a rest in his chair.

MY DAD IS A SUPERHERO

My Dad can heal any ouchie. When I fell off of the swing in our backyard, I landed on a stick and cut my hand.

My Dad put some medicine on the cut, and then he blew on it with his superhero powers.

Before I knew it, my cut did not hurt anymore.

I have been thinking.

Even if my Dad wasn't faster than a speeding bullet. Or stronger than a lion, or couldn't read my mind, have x-ray vision or sonic hearing.

Or even if he didn't know the answers to the super secret questions in the newspaper.

I think I'd still love him just the same, as much as he loves me.

A Note from the Author

To my dear readers:

Thank you so much for purchasing *My Dad Is A Superhero*. I really hope you and your kids enjoyed reading it as much I enjoyed writing it.

I appreciate that you chose to buy and read my book over some of the others out there. Thank you for putting your faith in me to help educate and entertain your children.

If you and your kids enjoyed *My Dad Is A Superhero* and you have a spare couple of minutes now, it would really help me out it if you would like to leave me a great review (even if it's brief) on Amazon. All these reviews really help me spread the word about my books and encourage me to write more and add more to the series!

If you'd like to read another one of the books from my Children's Books series, I've included some on the next page for you.

Warmest Regards,   *Lily Lexington*

Rhyming Books by Lily Lexington

My Dinosaur is Scared of Vegetables

If you like stories by Maurice Sendak, Jon Klassen, Dr Seuss and P D Eastman then you will love this beautiful tale told by Lily Lexington in her debut children's story.

Follow Jack and his cute dinosaur friend in his quest to avoid eating his vegetables.

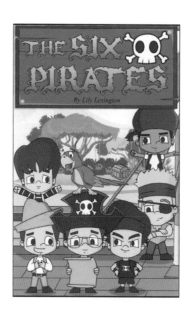

The Six Pirates:
A Rollicking and Rhyming Picture Book

If your child enjoys stories from authors like Jane Yolen, Kevin Henkes, Katherine Paterson or Patricia Polacco then your child will love this rollicking and rhyming sea adventure.

The six pirates have two big problems; they have run out of food and none of them can agree on where they should sail, let alone anything else. Will this be the end of the beloved six pirates or will the bickering buccaneers find their way to a new home?

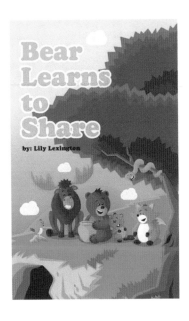

Bear Learns to Share

If your child enjoys stories like Winnie the Pooh or other stories by Maurice Sendak, Jon Klassen, Dr Seuss and P D Eastman then you will love this beautiful tale told by Lily Lexington in this children's story for kids both big and small.

Follow Bear with vibrant, colorful pictures as he plays with his friends in the forest and discovers what happens when he does not share.

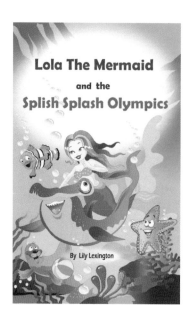

Lola the Mermaid
and The Splish Splash Olympics

If your child enjoys stories from authors like Kate DiCamillo, Cynthia Rylant, Mem Fox or Gary Paulson then your child will love this beautiful mermaid tale told by Lily Lexington in this children's picture story book complete with a valuable lesson.

Follow Lola the Mermaid with beautiful illustrations in her quest to win the gold medal for diving in the Splish Splash Olympics. Will she win the gold medal? Discover what happens in this fun tale.

My Dad Is A Superhero

Does your dad have x-ray vision or can he fly faster than a speeding bullet?

5 year old Sam is not like other boys, at least not with respect to his father, who is a superhero. "My Dad is a Superhero" is a fun tale that explores Sam's bond with his dad and his incredible super powers.

Told from the point of view of Sam, it is a fun story that ends on a warm fuzzy note that is just perfect for bedtime. Children will take delight in the amazing and varied super powers of Sam's dad and parents will take delight in some of the humor placed throughout the tale.

This book is a bedtime story for ages 2-6.

Pick up your copy today!

The Tale of
Luna the Moth

Luna feels different from her butterfly family. She wants to belong but
deep down she knows she is not the same as the other butterflies. Follow
Luna in her journey to find out who she is in the cute story for kids
both young and old.

The story ends with a great lesson about acceptance that all parents will resonate with.
- Beautiful, color illustrations that will captivate your young child.
- Rhyming lines help engage your child and sustain interest

Your younger children will enjoy the illustrations and sing-song tone of the
story while your older children will particularly like the rhyming story format.

*For more books, please visit www.LilyLexington.com or my author page at
www.amazon.com/author/lilylexington*

Book Availability

All of Lily's print books are available in digital format on the Amazon Kindle. Just go to your country specific Amazon website and search for Lily Lexington.

Lily's Works Translated

Lily's bestselling book; 'My Dad is a Superhero' has been translated into Spanish, German, French, Italian, Japanese and Portuguese. All of these books are available in digital version only on Amazon Kindle. To find them search for Lily Lexington on Amazon.com and browse through Lily's collection.

Made in the USA
Lexington, KY
02 June 2015